comix.

TOM'S PTERODACTYL

Colin West

Read about my brilliant uncle Tom and the strange umbrella he owns.

A & C Black • London

comix

356628

First paperback edition 2001
First published 2001 in hardback by
A & C Black (Publishers) Ltd
37 Soho Square, London, W1D 3QZ

ISBN 0-7136-5839-8

A CIP catalogue for this book is available from the
British Library.

Printed and bound in Spain by G. Z. Printek, Bilbao

CHAPTER ONE

Last year my mum and dad had a funny idea.
They decided to go away on what they called
their 'second honeymoon'. And I wasn't invited!

I didn't mind too much, to tell the truth. You see, we arranged for me to stay with my uncle Tom in Shrimpton-on-Sea.

Actually, he's my Great-great Uncle Thomas (on my mother's side). But he's plain Uncle Tom to me.

The following week we packed our bags and drove down to Shrimpton-on-Sea.

What a wonderful place!

SCREECH

Welcome one and all!

Uncle Tom greeted us warmly at the gate of his cottage.

My! You've grown!

So has your beard, Uncle.

Then Mum and Dad went off on their second honeymoon. They were returning to the same hotel they'd stayed in ten years ago!

Uncle Tom invited me inside...

We had tea in his tiny front room. Uncle Tom told me all about the local wildlife.

As we tucked into buttered scones, I asked an innocent little question...

Uncle Tom, what's the most unusual creature you've ever come across?

Walk this way, my lad.

My uncle leaned back in his chair and seemed lost in thought. Then a smile took over his face and he led me to the hallway.

'Now what do you see?' he asked with a twinkle in his eye.

10

The answer seemed simple enough: I could see an umbrella stand with an assortment of sticks.

But as I looked more closely at the brolly, what I thought was the handle (in the form of a bird's head) slowly turned to me and winked a beady eye.

I almost fell over with astonishment!
My uncle chuckled loudly. He clapped his hands
and the 'umbrella' came to life once more.

With a flutter of wings, the creature settled on
my uncle's outstretched arm.

My uncle chuckled again.

This is Terry and he's not a bird. He's a reptile who happens to fly.

You see, Terry is a Pterodactyl.

I could hardly believe my eyes and ears. Pterodactyls, I knew, had been extinct for millions or trillions of years. Yet this one looked live enough to me!

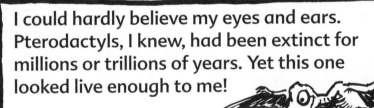

His wings are like well-worn leather and his eyes like glass marbles.

But how on earth had Uncle Tom found such a peculiar pet? Well, over a cup of cocoa, he told me the whole amazing story...

It seemed that my uncle had found an egg on a remote cliff top a few years earlier.

Goodness! What's this?

The egg had been preserved in soft mud for two hundred million years, Uncle Tom told me.

Which makes Terry two hundred million and three years old, I reckon.

I learned that my uncle placed the egg by the fireside and surrounded it with hot water bottles.

Egg-citing, isn't it?

After several weeks of this treatment, a sharp little beak pecked away from inside and out popped Terry!

My uncle had kept the little creature alive with a diet of insects and worms. He was soon a healthy fully-grown pterodactyl!

Fancy a nice, juicy earthworm?

Uncle Tom decided to keep his discovery a secret from the world. He didn't want Terry to be examined, x-rayed and experimented upon.

Pterodactyl Skeleton

That would be excruciating!

Uncle Tom looked serious for a moment.

In fact there are two people around here I'm particularly concerned about.

I was all ears as Uncle continued...

17

Uncle Tom heaved a sigh.

So you see, it's really important no one knows about Terry.

Don't worry, Uncle, your secret is safe with me.

That's good to know, my lad.

And so, apart from Uncle Tom, I was the only person in the whole wide world who knew about Terry. I felt really honoured!

We can take Terry out tomorrow and you can get to know each other.

Wow!

CHAPTER TWO

I hardly slept that night through excitement, and was up at the first sign of daybreak. Uncle Tom and Terry were up early too, and the three of us left for the trail along the cliff tops.

One thing bothered me, though.

'What if someone sees Terry with us?' I asked as the pterodactyl flapped about our heads. Uncle Tom chuckled loudly.

From a distance he looks just like a big bird...

...but if anyone does get too close, Terry does his impression of an umbrella.

At the sound of the word 'umbrella', Terry immediately flew back to us. He folded his wings and hung from my uncle's arm.

Terry's terrific!

He looked just like some old worn-out brolly! It was just as well, as right then two hikers came into view...

Just keep calm, my lad.

They passed by with a cheery greeting.

I'm sure they didn't suspect a thing!

'As you were, Terry,' Uncle Tom commanded when they were out of sight. The pterodactyl came to life once more and flapped about our heads.

That morning with Terry was terrific fun. We watched him take off when he felt a breeze come along...

...and then glide for a while on an air current...

...before doing loop-the-loops and flying upside down!

When Terry had had enough of the aerobatics, he gently landed on Uncle Tom's outstretched arm.

Well done, Terry.

Umbrella!

My uncle gave the command and Terry adopted his umbrella position.

Now it was safe to make our way down to the beach!

A few holiday-makers stared at us a little, but they could never have guessed our secret.

That's what we need – a beach umbrella!

We were all rather peckish now. We went to a snack bar and I slyly fed some of my hamburger to Terry.

We spent the afternoon exploring the rock pools, with Uncle Tom pointing out all sorts of wonders to me.

By the end of the day, the pterodactyl and I were firm friends.

'It's been fantastic!' I said as I sank into an armchair back at the cottage. Uncle Tom helped Terry settle in his umbrella stand, and the three of us prepared for a good night's rest.

CHAPTER THREE

The following day I was up early again. Terry was dancing on my shoulder as I sang 'Ten green bottles' (rather badly).

And if one green bottle should...

Suddenly I heard the sound of the latch on the gate.

CLUNK!

Turning round, I saw the postlady coming up the garden path! I quickly whispered the magic word.

Umbrella!

Terry at once leapt from my shoulder to my elbow, where he dangled casually.

'That was a neat trick!' the postie cried out, politely applauding me.

CLAP CLAP!

You should be in the circus with an act like that!

I breathed a sigh of relief as she handed me my uncle's mail.

That umbrella looked almost alive!

Terry couldn't resist winking an eye. I don't **think** the postlady noticed anything strange.

That's funny! I could have sworn that old brolly winked at me!

I took the letters in to my uncle.

Phew! That was close.

I see you've met Patsy the Postie.

I realised Uncle Tom had viewed the whole episode from a front window. Terry winked at me again and Uncle Tom chuckled to himself.

Now, who's for bacon and eggs?

Yes, please!

After a hearty breakfast the three of us went down to the beach.

Uncle Tom had promised me another surprise! He held Terry upside-down and slowly walked across the shore.

After a while, Terry's head twitched, and he started digging furiously with his beak. Before long, he unearthed a small coin!

Uncle Tom rubbed it on his sleeve...

Uncle Tom put the coin in his pocket, and repeated the procedure with Terry. In next to no time Terry came up with a rusty brooch...

It was incredible — Terry seemed to know almost instinctively where little objects might be buried just inches below the ground.

We had to keep away from some other treasure seekers in case they got curious about our odd 'metal detector'. They didn't seem to have as much success as us.

By the end of the day, we'd found half a dozen items — the brooch, two old coins, an arrow head, an old tin soldier (with a broken arm) and an ancient buckle for a belt.

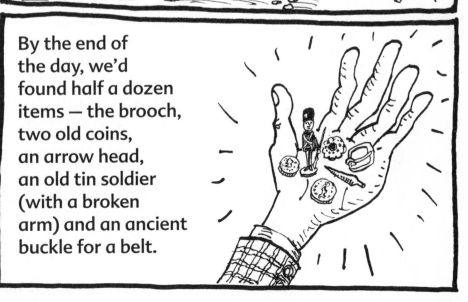

It had been another great day. But I couldn't help noticing two suspicious figures in the distance.

Look, Uncle, it looks like those two Nosy Parkers.

You could be right, my lad. We'd best be off.

Terry gave me his familiar wink and we made our way home.

Phew! That was another close shave!

CHAPTER FOUR

The following morning I learned another of Terry's funny tricks. I'd slept like a log that night and was still dreaming away at eight o'clock. But then I felt a sudden nipping at my toes.

I rubbed my eyes...

Apart from being a living alarm clock, Terry was also useful as a kitchen help. He placed dirty crockery in the sink ready for washing up.

It's true he **sometimes** broke the odd cup or saucer, but on the whole, he was surprisingly skilful.

Anyway, Uncle Tom didn't seem to mind the odd bit of broken crockery. That particular morning he was sweeping up a broken milk jug.

Terry seemed particularly impatient to go down to the shore with Uncle Tom and me. Not that I minded!

We might as well be off – before he does any more damage!

Come on, Terry.

So we left early, and I was surprised we weren't the first ones on the beach. There were already two people walking by the sea.

We did our best to ignore them and pushed out my uncle's rowing boat.

Uncle Tom had an important announcement to make...

What followed amazed me as much as Terry's treasure-hunting exploits.

Suddenly:

A moment later, Terry emerged with a mackerel in his beak.

GULP!

Then with a flick of his head, Terry promptly swallowed the fish. He repeated the whole performance three times, each time coming up with a larger fish than before.

When Terry had eaten his fill, he continued diving for more fish and Uncle Tom took them from his beak.

That evening we had a glorious fish supper. And it was all thanks to Terry!

I went to bed that night with dreams of shipwrecks and buried treasure to carry me through till next morning.

CHAPTER FIVE

Next day I still felt rather dozy. I happened to be by the door with Terry when the postlady called. I only **just** managed to say 'umbrella' in time.

I think I got away with it once more, and breathed another sigh of relief.

That umbrella looked even more alive than before!

As Patsy the Postie left, I noticed a postcard from my parents.

Ye Olde Honeymoon Hotel!

I must be seeing things.

So I excitedly joined Uncle Tom in the kitchen.

Mum and Dad are enjoying their second honeymoon.

Uncle Tom chuckled and served up breakfast.

44

When I was on my third piece of toast, I decided to ask Uncle Tom about an idea I had.

Uncle, you know how Terry likes finding hidden treasure underground?

Uncle Tom nodded as he munched his toast...

And you know how Terry likes diving for fish?

My uncle nodded again...

Well, why not combine the two activities — and have him dive for sunken treasure!

My uncle let out one of his loudest laughs. 'It sounds crazy enough to work!' he chortled.

Terry, who'd been warming his feet on the toaster, suddenly started flapping his wings madly, as though he understood our plans.

The three of us were soon down on the beach, where we took out Uncle Tom's rowing boat again. We had to be extra careful this time, as I'm sure I noticed a couple of people lurking behind the rocks.

We made sure we were a long way out so no one could see us. I held up Terry by his feet...

Uncle Tom rowed around for a while, but Terry didn't twitch a single twitch.

'Maybe there's nothing **to** detect,' said Uncle Tom.

When I was a younger man, I often went snorkelling in these parts, and I never came across any sunken treasure.

Let's call it a day then.

So rather sadly I hauled Terry aboard. Just then he started flapping about furiously.

Don't rock the boat!

48

Suddenly Terry clambered over the side and with a mighty splash disappeared underwater.

'Don't worry!' Uncle Tom reassured me.

That creature knows what he's doing.

I leaned over the side expectantly.

I wondered what could possibly be going on.

Suddenly Terry surfaced. And he had something glittering in his beak.

Wow! What's he got?

I helped Terry aboard and Uncle examined the object.

Good gracious!

'Is it precious?' I asked impatiently.

Well, it is to me!

I could hardly wait to hear why.

We rowed back to the shore triumphantly. Terry was so proud of himself, he was flapping about like mad as we walked along the beach...

But then from out of the caves stepped my worst nightmare — it was a couple I recognised immediately from my uncle's description — the two Nosy Parkers!

There was no time to utter the magic word 'umbrella'. But Terry was brilliant! He suddenly started flying round in circles and buzzing loudly.

I realised what he was up to. I stammered out a question...

Er, how do you like my model pterodactyl?

Primrose and Percy Parker were speechless.

Suddenly Terry stopped buzzing and made a spluttering sound.

He went into a spectacular nose dive and made a crash landing.

The Nosy Parkers started arguing with each other.

CHAPTER SIX

My week at Shrimpton-on-Sea went by really quickly. All too soon it was my last day. Uncle Tom was busy indoors, so I was making myself useful in the garden.

Even hanging out washing was good fun with Terry helping out with the pegs!

Thanks, Terry.

Then we all had tea in the garden. It was one of the hottest days of the year, and Terry basked in the sunshine while at the same time shading Uncle's face.

Halfway through the afternoon I heard a car sound its horn.

It was Mum and Dad back from their second honeymoon! Uncle Tom whispered 'umbrella' quickly. Terry hung from his elbow as I hugged my parents.

I fetched my bag before joining the others by the car.

I gave Terry a farewell pat on the head and whispered a message. Terry gave me one of his sly winks.

Then Uncle Tom shook me by the hand and pressed something into my palm.

I got in the car and looked at Uncle's gift.

It was the beautiful pocket watch! I held it to my ear and heard it ticking away. Uncle Tom had managed to mend it!

Then Mum and Dad joined me in the car, and we waved goodbye.

As the car pulled away, I watched until Uncle Tom and Terry were tiny dots in the distance.

We were soon out of Shrimpton-on-Sea.
'You know, Uncle Tom is a funny old chap,' Mum remarked...

Even on a lovely day like this he carries that old umbrella on his arm!

'Ah, but that's some umbrella!' I thought as I remembered my fantastic holiday with Uncle Tom's pterodactyl.